Wade got up.
"It is late," said Mom.
"But make your bed."

"I made my bed, Mom,"
said Wade.
But Wade had not
made his bed.

Wade ate and ran to
get the bus.

Wade came home on
the bus.
His Mom met him.

"Your bed was not
made," said Mom.

Mom and Dad had
made a rule.
"If your bed is not
made, Wade, you can
not ride your bike,"
said Dad.

Wade was sad.
It was late, so
Wade got into his bed.

As the sun came up,
Wade woke up and
made his bed.

Wade came home on
the bus and ran to
get his bike.

Mom came up to him.
"Your bed was not
made," said Mom.

"But I made my bed,
Mom," said Wade.
"It was not made,"
said Mom.

Wade ran up.
His bed was not made!

Wade made his bed.
As Wade sat, his pup
ran in and got up on
the bed.

His pup dug in the bed.
The pup made a big pile.
Mom came in.

"I did make my bed,"
said Wade.
"But the pup got up
and dug in the bed."

The pup had fun, but
Wade did not.
Wade had to make his
bed one more time.